700036284495

D0310460

For Alfie James Yarrow, born 27th June 2008.
With love, C.M. xxx

First published in Great Britain in 2009 by Boxer Books Limited.
www.boxerbooks.com

Text and illustrations copyright © 2009 Cathy MacLennan
Spooky Doo font copyright © 2009 Cathy MacLennan

A CIP catalogue record for this book
is available from the British Library upon request.

The illustrations were prepared using acrylic paints on blue kraft paper.
The text is set in Spooky Doo.

ISBN 978-1-906250-66-9

1 3 5 7 9 10 8 6 4 2

Printed in China

All of our papers are sourced from managed forests and renewable resources.

Spooky Spooky Spooky!

Cathy MacLennan

Boxer Books

Velvety,
velvety
bats . . .

And horrible howling cats.

Webby
webs

and spider
eggs . . .

Then lots and lots and lots of legs.

Rotten rats and bug-eyed flies, gobbling up the pumpkin pies.

Meander, meander,
slip slimy snails,

slithery slugs and silver trails.
Spooky spooky spooky!

Plants that climb
and plants that curl,
Wings that swoosh
and eyes that swirl.

Spooky spooky spooky!

The moon, the moon!
What's happened
to the moon?
It's dark,
it's dark,
it's very,
very dark!

SPOOKY SPOOKY SPOOOOOKY!

On come the lights

of the fireflies . . .

Then bright toothy smiles

and light-up eyes.

Out come the trick-or-treaters to play!

AWAY go
bats and cats,
spiders and rats,
owls and bugs,
snails and slugs.